The Best Christmas

Also in the Redwing Series

KIT   Jane Gardam
EARTHQUAKE   Ruskin Bond
TIGERS FOREVER   Ruskin Bond
MIDNIGHT PIRATE   Diana Hendry
ON THE NIGHT WATCH   Hannah Cole
THE MEETING POST   Lee Kingman
HETTY'S FIRST FLING   Diana Hendry
THE HAUNTING OF HEMLOCK HALL   Lance Salway
THE SHAPE-CHANGER   Julian Atterton
WE THREE KINGS FROM PEPPER STREET PRIME
   Joan Smith
YOUR GUESS IS AS GOOD AS MINE   Bernard Ashley
OUR HORRIBLE FRIEND   Hannah Cole
STAPLES FOR AMOS   Alison Morgan
KIT IN BOOTS   Jane Gardam

Lee Kingman

The Best Christmas

Illustrated by Janet Duchesne

Julia MacRae Books
a division of Franklin Watts

Text © 1986 Lee Kingman
Illustrations © 1986 Janet Duchesne
Originally published in the United
States of America, 1949, copyright by
Lee Kingman Natti.
This revised edition first published
in Great Britain 1986 by
Julia MacRae Books
A division of Franklin Watts
12a Golden Square, London W1R 4BA
and Franklin Watts, Australia,
14 Mars Road, Lane Cove, NSW 2066

British Library Cataloguing in Publication Data
Kingman, Lee
    The best christmas – (Redwing books)
    I. Title   II. Series
    813'.52 [J]   PZ7
    ISBN 0 86203 262 8

Phototypeset by Ace Filmsetting Ltd, Frome, Somerset
Printed and bound in Great Britain by
Garden City Press, Letchworth

Contents

1   Trouble for Christmas, 7

2   Erkki's Secret, 20

3   Hunting the Hemlock, 33

4   A Candle in the Window, 44

5   Surprises under the Tree, 55

1 Trouble for Christmas

"Christmas is coming!
    Christmas is coming!"

Erkki Seppala sang the words aloud as he
walked along the dark street. But the thoughts of
Christmas made him so burstingly happy inside
that even his little out-loud song sounded thin
and cold in the winter evening.

Why did Christmas always make him feel so
warm and excited? Was it the presents? Was it
the star and the tree at the church? Or was it
because all the family were home and they had
such a happy time together?

Erkki began running to keep warm. The road
went up the hill from the sea, and the freshly
salted wind rushed all around him, pushing at

him. But with Christmas coming, Erkki didn't mind the cold.

The wind pushed him on, faster and faster, until he was racing it. Up the hill they flew! At the top Erkki stopped and turned around. The wind was so strong it shut his eyes for a minute. Then he looked out towards the ocean. The sea was a cold grey-blue, but there was just a bit of colour to draw a line around the hills across Ipswich Bay where the sun had set. The sky was a great dark place and there was the first star winking in it.

It was a tiny faraway light that didn't seem half so real to Erkki as the big silver-tinsel star they would put on top of their Christmas tree! But now that Erkki saw the star in the sky, he made a wish as he had done every night since Thanksgiving. "Christmas is coming. Please let it be the best one I've ever had."

Even as he said the words, the wind threw them away. He turned quickly and ran home. The Seppala farmhouse looked as if it were trying to cuddle down among the apple trees and hide from the winter gales that howled in from the Atlantic

Ocean. Erkki flung open the door to the back kitchen that was used for a storeroom in winter and stamped in.

The dogs jumped up to meet him, and he had to play with them before he could take off his boots. He hung his coat and cap on a peg and went to open the door to the kitchen, the centre of everything for the Seppalas in the winter.

There was a big table covered with a red-checked cloth where they gathered for meals. In a corner by the huge black coal stove were two rocking chairs that were always busy. Mother or Father would sit there, or one of the older girls, holding a younger child to be fed, or comforted, or rocked to sleep. And sometimes the younger ones climbed in by themselves, to sit stiff-legged, boots just sticking beyond the edge of the chair, hands clutching the arms, rocking their bodies until they set the chair rocking, too.

Erkki knew the kitchen would be full of the homely smell of baking bread, or pies, or the friendly smell of stew. It was always full of people, too, even when it was just the family!

There were Mother and Father Seppala; tall grown-up Matti, who burst home from a trip on the stone barge as if he'd missed every minute with his family; slender blond Saima, who worked in a pastry shop in Gloucester; then round-faced, laughing Mikko, who had left school now he was sixteen, so he could work, too; and serious, quiet Aili, who was a big help to Mother now she was twelve; then came Erkki, who with ten whole years behind him felt much, much older than his seven-year-old brother, Arni; the twins, Elana and Eino, were five, and noisy; Lauri, who was three, was learning to keep out of everyone's way; but Anna, the baby, knew only that if she yelled loud enough with her strong year-old voice after a while someone would see what she wanted.

When they were all laughing or talking or singing at once it was like being at a party!

But tonight when Erkki opened the door with "Christmas is coming!" singing on his lips, the room was full of people and very quiet.

12

Mother was sitting in her rocking chair with her hands over her eyes and Father was patting her shoulder. Aili and Saima had their arms around each other and were crying. The younger children knew something was wrong. They were still and staring. Even Mikko's usual smile was gone.

"What's the matter?" asked Erkki.

"Matti's stone barge must be in trouble. She should have come into Boston two days ago," Mikko explained. "But she's missing."

The stone barge was a large boat which carried big pieces of granite from Cape Ann to Boston or New York. It sailed so slowly that the trip from Gloucester to Boston took several days.

"Matti said he'd be home in three or four days, and that would be the last trip until spring," Mother said.

Erkki didn't want to believe it. Not his big brother Matti, who told such wonderful stories! Not with Christmas coming! "He said he'd be

home for Christmas!'' was all Erkki could say.

Supper was the stillest meal Erkki had ever known, because no one felt like saying a word.

After supper Mother and Father sat in their chairs by the stove and rocked and rocked. Aili and Saima washed and wiped the dishes in the tiny sink room off the kitchen while Erkki and Arni carried them to the cupboards and put them away.

This was the time when Mother usually did her knitting. With ten children in the family, she didn't have time to knit more than one pair of mittens a year for each of them, so she gave the mittens to them at Christmas. The children never asked who the mittens were for, even though they watched each one grow. The surprise came on Christmas Eve when they took their presents off the tree – to see which pair of mittens belonged to each one. Mother would hang them on the tree, with the name hidden under a bow of yarn. In the thumb of each mitten was a shiny coin from Father. And last year Saima had saved some of her money and bought a candy cane to put in each mitten.

15

But Erkki saw that Mother wasn't knitting
tonight. When Lauri came and pushed his head
against her knees, she picked him up and rocked
him, as if she were trying to keep all children, big
and small, safe in her arms.

Erkki's thoughts kept returning over and over
to Christmas. Would they have a Christmas if
Matti didn't come home? He couldn't wait any
longer without knowing.

"When are you going out in the woods to find
our Christmas tree?" he asked Father.

"Why, it is almost Christmas, isn't it!" Father
seemed surprised. How could grown-ups be so
quiet about Christmas, when children waited all
year for it? "Let's see. Christmas is just two weeks
from tomorrow." He ruffled Erkki's fair hair until
it looked like a pile of beach straw. "Perhaps you
and Mikko could go with me the Saturday before
Christmas?"

Erkki's face shone with a smile. They would have a tree, and he would find it! He knew just what they wanted – a hemlock with tiny brown cones hidden in the green branches!

Mother stopped rocking, and Lauri's head flopped forward as he slept. "Why go to all that trouble?" she asked Father. "Without Matti – it just won't be Christmas!"

Erkki's thoughts stopped right where he heard Mother say *trouble*. Was Christmas a trouble to anyone? He always thought everyone was happy at Christmas – from the time of lighting the first candle for the window on Christmas Eve to blowing it out when they went to bed on Christmas night. Why, Christmas was wonderful! What was trouble about it?

Arni's big blue eyes stared hard at Mother. "No tree?" he whispered.

Elana's mouth was open, ready to cry loudly.

Eino said firmly the question he asked one hundred times a day anyway, but now it was important. "Why?"

Mother looked at them all, each one waiting for her to decide a most important thing. Erkki saw that Mikko had stopped trying to mend his skate and Aili and Saima were listening, too.

"I guess I forgot what Christmas means," said Mother. "It wouldn't feel right not to have Christmas, would it?"

"Oh no!" Smiles began to grow again.

"Of course we'll have a Christmas – and a tree." Mother was smiling again herself. "And we hope Matti's boat will be found by then and he'll be home."

She handed Lauri to Saima and reached into the knitting bag which always hung on the back of her chair, bumping softly as she rocked. Out came a pair of mittens and her fingers flashed away – red yarn, blue yarn, over and over.

Erkki yawned. The cold walk to the beach before supper had made him sleepy. He went upstairs to bed and his last awake thought was "Christmas is coming!"

2 Erkki's Secret

But when he awoke, shivering with cold, the next morning, the little 'Christmas-is-coming' song in his head was followed by another thought. If Matti didn't come home, there wouldn't be any *big* presents!

For three years, since Matti had worked on the stone barge, he bought the kind of presents that made Christmas exciting! Not that Erkki didn't like Mother's warm mittens and Father's shiny coins. He knew that with ten children to clothe and feed and keep warm Mother and Father couldn't buy them toys and games. Mother often said at Christmas, "You know our biggest package for each of you is our love."

But Matti bought his brothers and sisters the

20

present each one wanted most – toy wagons and sledges and games and dolls. The only toys they ever had came from Matti, and this year there might not be any! How disappointed the children would be.

Matti found out what each one wanted, and Erkki had said a new sledge, big enough to stay under him when he went coasting. The sledge he had just about took care of his stomach.

How could it be the best Christmas Erkki ever had? As he shivered in bed, he decided not to look forward to it at all. He didn't even want to crawl out of his nest of blankets and get dressed.

He ate his breakfast without saying much, and at school his mind wasn't in the room at all. After school he kicked a chunk of ice ahead of him all the way home, and didn't stop to look at the ocean once. Instead of hanging up his coat and cap, he dropped them on the floor of the store-room. What was the point of bothering? He kicked the cap into a far corner just as Mother came in with a basket of eggs.

"Erkki!" she said. "That cap won't last you another year if you don't take better care of it."

Erkki shrugged his shoulders. "I don't care."

"Christmas is coming," Mother reminded him.

"Yes," said Erkki. "But it won't be very good this year without Matti."

"Erkki." Mother put the eggs down carefully and turned Erkki around until he had to look up at her. She couldn't scold. Each of them had such a weight in his heart about Matti. She knew, too, how the children counted on his presents. "Even if Matti doesn't come home, we'll have a good Christmas somehow. Do you know why?"

Erkki shook his head.

"Because Matti would like it. He's a sort of special Christmas spirit for all of us. We'll do the things he'd like, and perhaps he'll be here anyway." Mother's voice was strong with hope and faith. "Now go and hang up your coat and cap, and then come in and have some hot milk."

As Erkki bent over to pick up his cap, he saw that it had landed on some boards he had never noticed before. Behind the boards were two little wooden wheels that looked as if they had come from a child's wagon. What could they be doing there, unless . . .

Suddenly Erkki had an idea! It was such an exciting idea that he gulped down his milk without waiting for it to cool. "Uff!" he spluttered. "I think I blistered my throat. I'm going out to cool it off."

He dashed into the storeroom and started to pick up the wheels and boards when Arni came in.

"What are you doing?" asked Arni.

Erkki knew if he said anything interesting, Arni would have to see all about it. So he just said, "Carrying some wood out to the barn. Want to help?"

"No." Arni skipped quickly away. Erkki hugged his armful of wood and wheels and hurried into the barn. There was a big workbench where Father made things for the house and repaired tools. It was almost dark, but Erkki lit the kerosene lamp and hung it safely out of the way.

23

He spread out the pieces. There were the two wheels, a long shaft with a crosspiece for a handle, and an old broomstick with ends whittled small enough to fit the holes in the middle of the wheels.

Erkki grinned happily. They were just what he needed to make a wagon for Arni for Christmas. Matti must have been planning to make it.

Erkki reached for a hammer and began nailing wooden pieces together to make a box. He whistled softly as he worked and didn't even notice how cold his feet were growing. The workbench was at the other end of the barn from the stall where the cow was munching her cud, with her warm breath steaming out into the cold room.

It took him a long time to work out how to fit the wheels onto the broomstick so they would turn without falling off. Maybe it wasn't quite what Matti intended, but when Erkki finished, he was very proud. The box fitted on the stick between the wheels. He fastened it tight and put on the long handle.

He heard Mother calling him to come to supper. How could he ever keep from telling them what he had been doing? And where could he hide the wagon so Arni wouldn't find it?

The light from the kerosene lamp shone on the wisps of hay falling over the edge of the loft. Tucked under the hay, no one would know it was there at all. Erkki carried the wagon up the ladder. He would paint it, and there would be a Christmas present for Arni.

Erkki put out the lamp and began whistling the little 'Christmas-is-coming' tune which had been in his head. Even his whistle had a secret sound as he closed the barn door.

There was that first star up in the sky, but Erkki didn't have time to stop and wish for the best Christmas he'd ever had.

"Where have you been, Erkki?" Arni wanted to know, as he came into the kitchen for supper.

"Just out," said Erkki. But his face suddenly put on such a large grin that he had to bite his tongue to keep from laughing.

Erkki took himself and his secret to bed early, because it kept popping up in his mind and he *did* want to talk about it. But before he went to sleep he tried to think of all the things the children had said they wanted, and how he could make them. He didn't have money to buy anything. He would have to find red paint for the wagon – and some wood to make a little train. And how could he ever make a doll for Elana!

As Christmas came nearer, Erkki hunted around to see if Matti had left other hints of things he planned to make, but he couldn't find any.

He hunted for paint, too. He found just enough to do the wagon wheels red, but there was a lot of black paint, so he painted the box with that.

The wagon looked handsome with its shiny black body and red wheels, like the little quarry engine that pulled the stone cars.

But it ought to have some gold curlicues to be like the engine, so Erkki found some yellow paint and a small brush and painted very swoopy curlicues around the top of the box. And since all engines have names, he wrote *Granite Express*. The letters were a little wobbly, but the name was grand. Erkki was so afraid Arni would find the present while the paint was drying that he spent most of the time in the barn shooing Arni away.

Arni, however, was hurt by all Erkki's secret hurrying and scurrying. When Erkki came into the storeroom at dark, he could hear Arni complaining to Mother in the kitchen. "I'm too big to play with the little ones, Mother," he said. "And Erkki won't let me play with him at all."

"Erkki seems to be very busy," said Mother.

"Yesterday he grabbed one of those round oatmeal boxes away from me," said Aili. "He just shook it to see if it was empty and then he walked off with it. I was only going to throw it away."

Erkki, in the dark storeroom, chuckled. The oatmeal box was going to be very useful.

"And what was he going through your scrap bag for, Mother?" Saima asked. "He told me Mikko asked him to find cleaning rags for his gun, but he had some pieces from my old velvet jacket and some embroidered stuff."

Erkki put his hands over his mouth so he wouldn't laugh out loud. Wouldn't they all be surprised!

"I didn't ask him for any rags," Mikko said.

30

"My, my!" Mother sounded surprised, but pleased. "Erkki is being even more mysterious than Matti at Christmas!"

With Matti's name, a silence pushed into the room. When Erkki came into the kitchen, they all looked worried.

"It's ten days now, isn't it," asked Aili, "since the stone barge was missing?"

Mother sat down heavily in her rocking chair. But Anna came bumping over the floor and held out her arms. So Mother picked her up and rocked her, while the older girls put supper on the table.

When Father came home, everyone looked up and asked the same question without even saying it out loud. Father just shook his head.

3 Hunting the Hemlock

Next morning Father opened the door to Erkki's little room and said, "Come on! Get up. We're going to the woods."

Erkki said sleepily, "What for?"

"For the Christmas tree."

Erkki jumped out of bed. Was it that close to Christmas already! Only four more days to Christmas Eve?

As he pulled on his clothes, he listed the things in his mind that he had finished. Arni's wagon and toys for the twins and Lauri and Anna. But he hadn't thought of anything for Aili and Mikko and Saima. And, most of all, Mother and Father. Matti would be sure to have something for all of them!

While Erkki ate his oatmeal, Mikko and Father were sharpening the axe on the grindstone. He could hear the whining sound it made. As soon as he finished, he slapped on his cap and dashed out the door.

"Erkki, come back," called Mother. "Don't you know how cold it is outdoors?"

Standing still long enough to find out, Erkki realized that the air made the end of his nose tingle and his ears prickle. The winter wind shoved right through his jacket as if it couldn't wait to go around him. He stuck his hands in his pockets and said, "It's not cold."

"Come back." Mother pulled him inside the storeroom door. "Here's an old winter shirt. And here's a scarf to tie around the neck. And here . . ." She reached for the knapsack packed with sandwiches and hung it on his back. "How grown-up you look with that knapsack!"

In spite of the large shirt flapping about his
knees, Erkki marched happily out to join the
Christmas-tree hunters, and off they went.

The first light snowfall of the year had been
tossed aside by the wind and melted by the sun.
Only the shaded hollows of the woods still held
snow. The ground was clear and hard.

They walked quickly, as it was four or five
miles from the Seppala farmhouse to the wild and
lonely stretch of land called Dogtown Common.

35

Erkki had to take long strides to keep up, and no one talked. If he opened his mouth, the air rushing down his throat was too cold to swallow. By the time they came out of the woods at the edge of Dogtown, his head was pounding and he had to gasp for breath.

Father looked at Erkki in surprise. "I was thinking about last year when Matti came with me, and I forgot you haven't the longest legs in this family. Why didn't you tell us to stop a minute?"

Erkki couldn't say anything, but he grinned.

Mikko said, "Let's just keep on walking slower."

"Now's the time to look for hemlocks," Father reminded them.

So they walked on, keeping near the woods and searching for a good tree.

At last they found a perfect tree about ten feet high, with lots of tiny brown cones.

"Now," said Father, "let's eat our lunch. Then we'll cut down the tree."

In the shelter of a large rock the sunlight took the sting from the winter wind, and they enjoyed the sandwiches Mother had packed in the knapsack.

"How I wish," Father began, "I had more time to spend with you boys in the woods. I'd like to find some apple or cherry branches, too, so I could carve some new knife handles."

38

"I remember when you were always carving things," said Mikko. "You made me a toy boat once."

"So I did," said Father. "But even if I had time to carve now, I wouldn't have time to go and find the wood to begin with." Father sighed.

"I wish you had time to teach me to carve," said Mikko.

In the winter sunlight, Erkki saw his father's face was full of lines he'd never noticed in the lamplight of dark winter evenings. How old he looked. Yet Father went on, "I'm still a young man."

Erkki stared at him. What a lot of new ideas he had lately! First, Christmas was trouble, and now Father said he was still young! Did Father still dream about the things he'd like to do – the way Erkki did – and did Father still look forward to Christmas?

"Do you think Christmas is the most important day in the year?" Erkki asked.

Father's blue eyes twinkled. "Well – yes," he said.

"But we never give you any presents." Erkki suddenly wondered why Father thought it was important.

"Oh yes, you do," Father told him. "When I see all of you happy, with your eyes shining because your hearts are full of joy, what more could a father ask?"

"I should think you'd want lots of things," Erkki said slowly.

Father laughed. "Wait until you grow up! Besides, Christmas isn't just to get presents. It's a birthday for the Christ Child. And it's the spirit of giving that counts."

Mikko jumped up impatiently. "Let's get this tree cut down, or Christmas will be here before we get it home."

Erkki announced, "I'll cut down the tree."

"Oh, *Erk!*" said Mikko. "You couldn't even make a dent in it." He picked up the axe and started towards the tree.

"Wait a minute," said Father. "We'll all cut it down." He took the axe and gave it to Erkki. "Give it a cut."

Erkki swung the axe as manfully as he could, while Mikko and Father dodged away in a hurry. The blade bit into the tree and there was a white scar in the trunk. Erkki was so excited he didn't mind when Father hastily reached for the axe. He and Mikko took turns.

"The tree will fall in that clear space," Father said. "Erkki, come over here. You can give it another blow or two now."

Erkki whacked with all his strength and "Crrrreak!" the tree bent slowly towards the clearing. With another whack and a louder "Crrrrrrreeeeak!" it fell over.

"Good!" said Father. "Now, if Erkki will take the knapsack, Mikko and I will carry the tree."

They lifted it carefully. A few of the cones fell off, and Erkki picked them up without thinking very much of what he was doing. As he followed Father and Mikko through the woods, he made a game out of picking up more cones as they fell, until his knapsack held quite a few.

"We'll put the tree in the barn till Christmas Eve," Father said as they reached home.

Erkki dumped the pine cones onto the workbench.

"What are you going to do with those?" Mikko asked. "Glue them back on the tree?"

Erkki laughed. "No." What a silly idea. But his eye fell on the yellow paint can, and he had a much better idea. "I'll be in later on," he told them.

When Erkki woke the next morning, he knew what he could give Father for Christmas! He slipped out of bed and dressed warmly.

In the kitchen he helped himself to the oatmeal Mother had cooked all night on the stove. He found the knapsack, and as soon as the sun was really up and about in the sky, he started off.

It was so cold that his breath made clouds around him as he walked. But when he came back at noontime, and hid the knapsack in the barn, he had Christmas presents for Father and Mikko and Mother.

43

4 A Candle in the Window

On Tuesday the snow fell so heavily that all they could see from the windows were swirling, whirling flakes. When Erkki went out with Father to feed the animals, they could barely find their way from house to barn. Except for the lonely cries of the foghorn, warning ships from the rocks in the blinding storm, everything was so still and silent that Erkki shivered.

"It feels as if everything is waiting for something," he told Father.

"We are," said Father. "We are."

If only Matti would come home safely! Even in the kitchen, with the tea-kettle whispering steamily on the stove, the sound of the foghorn seemed to fill the whole room.

44

But late in the afternoon the storm stopped. The sky cleared, and all the Seppalas pelted out of the house to stretch and run before supper. As they watched, the sun began to sink over Ipswich Bay, and the snow-shining hills gleamed with such a brightness that they could hardly look.

Mother stood in the doorway. Her worried look had gone. "A sunset like that must mean something," she said.

When Erkki woke the next morning, he had almost forgotten it was the day before Christmas! He lay in bed for a minute trying to work out how he could put the presents from Matti under the tree to surprise everyone when they came back from church.

That evening the kitchen was sweet with the smell of baking coffee bread and mince and squash pies. When the sun set and the darkness crept in across the sea, they all went into the kitchen.

Erkki took the white candle Mother handed him, and after Mikko helped him melt one end and set it in a saucer, he lit it and gave it to Arni to set in the kitchen window.

It was a brave little light, flickering against the steamy windowpanes. Erkki thought of the wishes he made on the first evening star. "Oh, please!" he begged inside himself. "Make this the best Christmas we've ever had. Let Matti come home."

Suddenly Mikko tipped back his head and started singing. They all joined in, until the kitchen seemed to whirl with happy sounds and delicious smells from the oven. Erkki felt his heart beat faster. It was beginning to feel like Christmas!

One by one, following Father, with Mother carrying Anna, they marched out the kitchen door, grabbing up coats and scarves as they passed through the storeroom and out to the barn.

Father and Erkki lifted up the Christmas tree, while Mikko led them in an extra loud, extra joyful chorus for the pleasure of the cow and horse.

Then Father and Erkki carried the tree so carefully that not a tiny cone dropped off. Into the living room they took it, while Mikko ran back to the barn for a pail of sand. Then they stuck the trunk in the bucket and pushed the tree up tall and straight.

"Oh," cried Arni. "The top just touches the roof!"

"Where's the star?" cried Aili. The girls took a chair into the closet so they could reach the box of ornaments Matti usually lifted down.

"There's the star!" Erkki said. Father stood on a chair to slip its wire over the top of the tree.

Mother came in with the ten pairs of mittens and went quietly round the tree, hanging them here and there. None of the children would think of looking to see whose mittens were whose until they came back from church!

Saima came in with her paper bag full of candy canes and put one in each mitten, while Father was busy poking his shiny coins into the thumbs. Aili and Mikko took out the strings of paper chains the children had made last year.

When they finished, they stepped back to look.

"It's lovely, children," said Mother.

Father cleared his throat, and then didn't say anything.

Mikko kicked his boots together and whistled softly.

Arni and the twins and Lauri didn't say much – they just looked at the star and the tree.

But Erkki knew they were all thinking that their Christmas was all on the tree now. Matti wasn't here to surprise them all with presents he would sneak under the tree while they were at

church. Erkki wanted to grin because of his
secret, but no one seemed to be smiling. They
would rather have had Matti there without
presents than all the presents in the world.

"Oh," Mother said suddenly, "we'll have to
hurry, or we'll be late for church."

Outside the front door Father had lined up the
two big double-runner sledges. "Mikko, you pull
one and take the twins and Lauri. I'll take Arni
and Erkki and Aili on the other."

When they came to the top of the hill, Father
called, "Shall we coast to church?"

Mother laughed. "How else do you think you
could get those sledges down the hill without
coasting? It's not very dignified, but it's
Christmas Eve."

That was all Father and Mikko needed. With a
push they were off down the hill, and the wind
carried their laughing shouts back to Mother and
Saima who followed.

51

Before, Erkki had always enjoyed the Christmas Eve service, but tonight he was anxious to get home before the others, and put the presents around the tree.

After the service in the church, the families gathered in a big room downstairs where Santa Claus gave little bags of candy to the children. But Erkki didn't want to stay even for that. He told Mikko, "I've got to go home. I forgot something." He dashed out before Mikko could ask him any questions.

Except for the Christmas candle glowing in the kitchen window, the house was dark. Erkki fumbled for the door latch, and felt his way into the dark storeroom. Suddenly he had a feeling that someone else was in the room with him. There was a special quietness and darkness about one corner that made it seem alive!

But he didn't have time to worry about it. He found the lantern and lit it. Then he ran out to the barn. Arni's little wagon was still under the hay with the other things he had made. He carried them carefully down the ladder and into the house.

In the living room he knelt by the Christmas tree and put the presents under its branches. He looked at them happily, until he remembered that he hadn't put names on any of the presents. Quickly he found paper and pencil and printed them out.

He started to write 'From Matti.' But then he was afraid they would think that Matti had come safely home, and it would be so awful to find that he hadn't.

Yet he didn't write 'From Erkki,' because he was doing it for his brother. Then he spread out the gifts under the tree and placed the right name on each.

If he hurried, he might get back to the church before anyone missed him. He buttoned his coat and ran down the hill so fast that he almost pitched head first into a snowbank at the bottom.

5 Surprises under the Tree

Mikko and Father returned home slowly, the sledges weighted down heavily with children. When they reached the house, a quietness seemed to have come upon them all. They stood around uncertainly, until at last Father pushed open the door and sent them in. "You'll be cold. Go on in."

Erkki, standing first on one foot and then on the other, thought they would never go inside. He knew they were all missing Matti, but he could hardly wait for them to discover the presents.

He stepped on Arni's foot and nearly knocked Lauri flat, trying to rush into the living room first. This was the most exciting Christmas he had ever had!

As they gathered around the tree, Erkki realized they weren't expecting anything but the usual mittens. No one looked under the tree.

When Father started taking the mittens off, pair by pair, and handing them out, saying, "Now here's a beautiful present," Erkki could hardly sit still.

Then Lauri crawled under the tree and squealed. Erkki popped down on his knees to see that he didn't put his hand on the wrong toy and then refuse to part with it.

In a minute the whole family were peering under the branches, and the noise of discovery burst out happily.

"Look at the little train!"

"And the doll!"

"And the wagon!"

56

Erkki saw Mother straighten up and look hopefully around the room, and the others, too. Where was Matti?

In the silence that fell as they wondered, Erkki's voice sounded small and lonely. "I thought they're what Matti would want to do, so they're really from him."

"You made them!" Mother shook Erkki lovingly. "Oh, Erkki! What a happy Christmas you've made us."

"Did you really make this wagon?" Arni wanted to know, as he pulled the *Granite Express* over the carpet.

Erkki nodded. There was so much noise and excitement, he couldn't think of what to say to anyone. Mother and Father had to see each thing and admire it. There was Arni's gay wagon, and a little-boy wagon made the same way, but much, much smaller, for Eino.

Saima laughed when she found the velvet ball with Anna's name on it. "Here's my old jacket!"

She held it out to Anna, who squashed it to herself and hugged it contentedly. "Was that what you wanted to borrow a needle and thread for, Erkki?"

He laughed. "My fingers are still sore from sticking the needle into them."

The rest of the velvet had gone into a handsome dress for Elana's doll. To be sure it was not a very good doll. The body was made of sticks nailed together so that it wouldn't move at all. But the head was made of a little old rubber ball on which Erkki had painted a face. And, best of all, the doll had a house made of an old oatmeal box. Erkki had cut spaces for windows and painted a red front door. Elana was already playing house, and Erkki could see the rubber doll face staring out of the oatmeal-box window.

For Lauri there was the toy train made of blocks of wood, with a long string so Lauri could pull it on journeys.

"You didn't see your presents!" Erkki said suddenly.

Mother and Father and Saima and Aili and Mikko looked surprised. "For us, too?" they asked.

Erkki handed Aili and Saima little bracelets made of strings of tiny hemlock cones painted yellow.

"Oh, Erkki! They're beautiful!" they said.

He handed Father and Mikko bundles of sticks roughly tied together. "These don't look like much," he said, "but they're apple and cherry branches, so you can do some carving."

"That's great!" said Father. "I never would have time to hunt for them myself."

"Now you can teach me how to carve," said Mikko happily.

To Mother, Erkki handed a glass bowl he had found dusty and deserted at the back of a cupboard. In it he had put soft mosses and lichens from the woods, with some little red berries to brighten it.

Suddenly Arni, who had been poking about at the back of the tree, called out, "Hey, whose sledge is this?"

"Sledge!"

Erkki turned quickly to look. He hadn't made any sledge but he had wanted one so badly! Sure enough, Arni was dragging a handsomely varnished and sparkling Flexible Flyer from behind the tree. There was a tag tied to the top and Erkki pounced on it.

It read, 'To Erkki – from Matti!'

"But – how . . ." began Erkki.

The door to the hall was suddenly pulled open and a large and happy young man stood there; he called, "Merry Christmas, everyone!"

"Matti, Matti!"

"Oh, Matti!"

In a second he had Mother in his arms, and Father was clapping him on the back. The children were dancing around, with the little ones reaching for his hands and trying to climb up his legs.

"Are you all right?"

"What happened?"

"When did you come home?"

"Where have you been?"

"One at a time, one at a time!" Matti said. He popped Mother into a chair and sorted out the children until he could sit down, with Lauri and Elana and Eino all in his lap at once.

"I've just been out to sea, that's all, so I couldn't get word to you. We were driven off our course after our rudder broke. We drifted for three or four days and finally another boat sighted us. She helped tow us back to Boston, but it took a long time to get there. I just came in to Gloucester this afternoon."

"Oh, Matti," said Mother. "We know what Christmas really is – to have you home again."

62

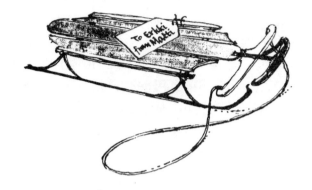

"It took me a little while to get here from
Gloucester, and I'd just come into the house to
surprise you, when I realized you were all at the
church. Then I heard someone come into the
storeroom after me, and I thought it was a
burglar. So I waited to pounce on him, and it was
Erkki being very mysterious."

"I thought someone was there!" exclaimed
Erkki.

"Anyway," said Matti, "you looked as if you
were carrying out surprises, so I just watched.
After you ran out, I looked at the presents under
the tree. You're a wonderful boy, Errki!"

Everyone talked at once about Erkki, until he couldn't seem to see anything but the copper toes shining on his boots.

"But you didn't have anything under the tree, so I just hid your sledge behind it. And I had some fun watching you through the crack in the door!" Matti chuckled. "I brought a few more things for the younger ones, because I didn't know I was going to have such a smart boy taking my place. But they're all shop-bought. Not half so nice as the things Erkki made. They're out in the hall."

The children scrambled to the hall and brought in the packages. There were games and shop dolls and toys. But somehow, grand as they were, the ones that meant the most were the ones Erkki had made.

"You know what?" Erkki said, as he blinked up at the silver-tinsel star on the tree. "This is the *best* Christmas I've ever had!"